This igloo book belongs to:

....

igloobooks

Published in 2019
by Igloo Books Ltd
Cottage Farm
Sywell
NN6 0BJ
www.igloobooks.com

GOL002 0519
4 6 8 10 9 7 5
ISBN 978-1-78440-729-2

Illustrated by Alex Paterson
Written by Melanie Joyce

Designed by Matthew Ellero
Edited by Will Putnam

Printed and manufactured in China

What Pirates Really Do

igloobooks

Oh, it's such a **jolly** life for pirates...

... sailing on the **sea!**

There are **swashbuckling** island adventures...

... and chests chock-**full** of **gold**.

There are **soft** and **cuddly** knitting classes.

... when the weather's cold.

By day, the pirates sail their ship...

... and **raid** along the coast.

But **relaxing** in the evenings is what they like **the most.**

Fearless pirates fight
sea monsters...

... and live on salty kippers.

Back at home, they put on pyjamas...

... and their best fluffy slippers.

Sometimes other **fierce** pirates come along...

... to pick a
fight.

Then everyone goes home,
snuggles up...

... and says, "Goodnight!"